MR. MEN LITTLE MISS

go Dancing

Roger Hargreaves

Original concept by
Roger Hargreaves

Written and illustrated by
Adam Hargreaves

EGMONT

Little Miss Star, as you may or may not know, was always looking for ways to become famous.

She longed for fame like Mr Greedy longed for cream buns.

So, she was very excited when she read the poster all about the dance competition to be held at the Grand Opera House in town.

There and then she decided she would become a famous dancer.

And to add to her excitement she read that the competition was to be televised.

"I'll be on telly!" she cried, clapping her hands in glee.

After entering the competition her next step was to find a dancing partner.

Who should it be?

Mr Tall? Tall and elegant, but maybe too tall!

Mr Strong? Strong and athletic, but maybe too strong!

Mr Cool? Cool and energetic, but maybe too cool!

And then she had the perfect idea.

The perfect person.

Mr Perfect!

And he couldn't wait to perfect a new skill. Practice makes perfect!

Little Miss Star and Mr Perfect spent many long hours rehearsing their dance steps. All the while only one thought filled Little Miss Star's mind. "I'm going to be famous!"

By the day of the competition they had perfected their dance routine.

And they had chosen wonderfully striking outfits.

The perfect outfits to stand out on television.

Little Miss Star and Mr Perfect turned up at the Grand Opera House on the evening of the competition.

It was quite an occasion.

All the other competitors were there. There was a huge audience. The TV cameras were recording. And the judges were seated at the judging table.

And who were the judges?

They were Mr Cheerful and Little Miss Sunshine and Mr Fussy and Little Miss Splendid.

Mr Cheerful was all fun and energy.

Little Miss Sunshine was all smiles and happiness. Mr Fussy
was busy arranging his score cards in a precise pile.

And Little Miss Splendid was busy being splendid!

The competition started with Little Miss Quick and Mr Slow.

They danced the foxtrot which involved a slow, slow, quick, quick, slow step combination.

Mr Slow was very good at the slow steps and Little Miss Quick was very good at the quick steps.

Surprisingly this meant they kept exact time!

The judges then held up their score cards.

Little Miss Sunshine awarded them ten out of ten.
Mr Cheerful gave them a seven.

Little Miss Splendid scored them a six.
And Mr Fussy … held up a one!

Fussy old Mr Fussy.

The next couple on the dance floor were
Little Miss Somersault and Mr Tickle
dancing what they called the
Tickle Tango.

It was a mesmerising tangle of arms and legs that somehow worked.

The audience clapped and cheered their admiration.

Three of the judges were on their feet.

It was a ten from Little Miss Sunshine and an eight from Little Miss Splendid and Mr Cheerful.

And Mr Fussy?

Oh dear, it was another one.

Which deserved a tickle!

Little Miss Star and Mr Perfect watched from the side, feeling more nervous by the minute.

The competition was in full flow.

The Little Miss Twins danced the two step in seamless unison.

Poor Little Miss Fun endured Mr Clumsy's clumsy feet treading on her toes.

And Mr Jelly was a jittery wreck dancing to Little Miss
Scary's version of the Jitterbug!

Little Miss Sunshine proved to be far too nice to give all the couples anything but ten out of ten.

And there was no pleasing Mr Fussy, who never budged from a one out of ten.

So, it fell to Little Miss Splendid and Mr Cheerful to make a competition of it.

With only one couple yet to dance, Little Miss Naughty and Mr Mischief were the surprising leaders with their lively samba.

It was finally Little Miss Star and Mr Perfect's turn on the dance floor.

They took their place under the spotlight.

The TV cameras zoomed in on them.

And the music started.

They began perfectly.

Little Miss Star was filled with high hopes.

What could go wrong?

Well, what did go wrong was Little Miss Naughty and Mr Mischief's desire to win. That very naughty pair secretly put itching powder in Little Miss Star and Mr Perfect's costumes!

As Little Miss Star began her first pirouette the itching powder took effect. They squirmed and twitched and scrabbled and scratched their itchy way around the ballroom.

They desperately tried to keep their composure, but it was hopeless.

It was a disaster.

Finally, they collapsed in an itching heap on the floor. The TV cameras had followed their every shudder and stumble.

The judges sat opened mouthed as the music finished.

Poor Little Miss Star and Mr Perfect.

No points!

They both went home feeling very disappointed.

Mr Perfect had to admit that practice didn't always make perfect.

All Little Miss Star's hopes of fame were ruined.

However, the next morning she got quite a surprise.

When she opened the newspaper, her picture was on the front page.

When she turned on the television, she was the main news story.

And it was the same on the radio and across the internet.

The disastrous dance had made headlines around the world.

She was famous!

Although, not famous for quite the reason she had hoped for. But, all the same, she was famous!

And so was Mr Perfect.

Although, he was not so happy.

Not so happy to be famous for something quite so imperfect!